James W. Alexander

Bring me up Samuel

AF135734

Anatiposi

James W. Alexander

Bring me up Samuel

Reprint of the original.

1st Edition 2023 | ISBN: 978-3-38230-550-5

Anatiposi Verlag is an imprint of Outlook Verlagsgesellschaft mbH.

Verlag (Publisher): Outlook Verlag GmbH, Zeilweg 44, 60439 Frankfurt, Deutschland
Vertretungsberechtigt (Authorized to represent): E. Roepke, Zeilweg 44, 60439 Frankfurt, Deutschland
Druck (Print): Books on Demand GmbH, In de Tarpen 42, 22848 Norderstedt, Deutschland

BRING ME UP SAMUEL.

BY

JAMES W. ALEXANDER, D.D.

"Whom shall I bring up unto thee?" And he said, "Bring me up
Samuel." 1 SAMUEL 28 : 11.

NEW YORK :

ANSON D. F. RANDOLPH,

No. 683 BROADWAY.

1859.

THIS SERMON,

AMONG THE LAST PREACHED BY ITS AUTHOR,

IS NOW GIVEN

TO THE PEOPLE FOR WHOM IT WAS ORIGINALLY PREPARED,

AS A MEMENTO OF THEIR PASTOR,

AND AN EXPRESSION

OF THE ABIDING AFFECTION OF

E. C. I.

BRING ME UP SAMUEL.

1 Samuel, 28 : 11.

——   &

We feel the freshness of the oriental and almost patriarchal scene, when the young and valiant son of Kish is sent out of Benjamin to seek the asses which had strayed. "He was a choice young man and a goodly, and there was not among the children of Israel a goodlier person than he: from his shoulders and upward he was higher than any of the people." The interview with the maidens near the well, and the introduction

to the Seer, are indelibly impressed upon
our memory. From that day the prophet
Samuel became, not only his mentor, but his
guardian angel, God's special messenger,
and afterwards his stern rebuker. Thus it
sometimes happens in our less important
lives, that the merest casualty brings us
acquainted with the person whose thread of
life is thenceforward to be closely twisted
with our own. In those days of youthful
simplicity and innocent surprise, Saul was
no doubt deeply under the influence of religious feeling. The shudder of reverential
awe had not worn away under custom in
sinning. He heard with astonishment his
designation as the deliverer of Israel; and
bowed his head with humble thoughtfulness
to the great anointing. He even became,
soon after, a sharer in prophetic gifts, which

were not confined to men of real inward holiness. More nearly still was he brought into hallowed connection with the prophet, when the venerable man, amidst the many thousands of Israel, brought him forth from his hiding, and said, "See ye him whom the Lord hath chosen, that there is none like him among all the people."

Religion was the prevalent spirit on the coronation-day, when "they sacrificed sacrifices of peace-offerings before the Lord; and there Saul and all the men of Israel rejoiced greatly." During all his early reign and successes, the young king was evidently under the guidance of Samuel, who continued to convey to him those counsels of God, by which even the monarch was to be governed under the theocracy. But pride led to presumption, and his conduct soon showed that

it was not his purpose to govern in the fear
of the Lord. Now the plot begins to thick-
en and take on darker colors. Saul, amidst
his host, insults the prophet by impatiently
offering sacrifice before his arrival. Samuel pronounces the awful words : "But now
thy kingdom shall not continue . . . because
thou hast not kept that which the Lord
commanded thee." Then follows a succes-
sion of disobediences and disasters. He
who had led Israel to victory suffers defeat
after defeat, intermingling with these the
transgression of express commands. In almost every one of these, Samuel appears in
the crisis of the dark hour, to frown on the
sin and to denounce vengeance. He who
as a little boy, girded with a linen ephod,
was sent to aged Eli with messages of re-
buke, is still the herald of divine judgment,

coming again and again upon the stage.
Again the God of his mother Hannah
had appeared unto him in vision, after the King's sparing of the Amalakite.
"Stay," said Samuel, "and I will tell thee
what the Lord hath said to me this night. .
. . . When thou wast little in thine own
sight, wast thou not made head of the tribes
of Israel. . . . Behold, to obey is better
than sacrifice, and to hearken than the fat
of rams. For rebellion is *as the sin of
witchcraft,* and stubbornness is as iniquity
and idolatry. Because thou hast rejected
the word of the Lord, he hath also rejected
thee from being King."

The effect of this reproof was not affront,
but horror. He confesses, he entreats, he
asks for the prophet's prayers, he seizes
upon his garment to prevent his going

away, so that the skirt of the mantle rent; upon which Samuel said, " The Lord hath rent the kingdom of Israel from thee this day and hath given it to a neighbor of thine, that is better than thou." Thus God does not leave the sinner unwarned, but meets him at every new turning even of his road of apostasy. This meeting at Gilgal closes the earthly connection of the king and the prophet. The point had been reached when reproof is no longer endurable. " Then Samuel went to Ramah, and Saul went up to his house to Gibeah of Saul. And Samuel came no more to see Saul until the day of his death ; nevertheless, Samuel mourned for Saul."

It is an affecting moment. We see their paths separating at this point. We observe on which side the union ceases. 'Samuel came no more to see Saul, until the day of his death.' We behold one going off into deeper iniquities and blacker clouds of peril and despondency, and the other seeking an old age of solitude, to lament over his fallen son. 'Nevertheless, Samuel mourned for Saul.' Last interviews of this kind are very touching. When God separates us from those who have been our chief advisers, who more than all other mortals have made us feel our sins, it is like taking away another barrier between us and ruin. It is related of *Samuel Finley*, that his influence was so great, by his faithful preaching, upon an intemperate man in his congregation, that this person was restrained for years from the excesses of his darling sin. At length Finley died. The news was brought to the parishioner, who exclaimed, 'My guardian is gone and I am lost,' and immediately re-sumed his intoxication and died the drunk-ard's death.

Even that ministry which we deem too austere, and under which we wince, sarcas-tically declaring it too heavenly for our worldly minds, is nevertheless a blessing, and keeps us from secret sins, and the taking of it away from us is sometimes a premoni-tion of wrath. 'Samuel came no more to see Saul until the day of his death.' But I suppose his stately figure and reproachful face often visited the king, amidst the sleep-less hours of his palace and the dreary watches of the battle-field. The impression made on the soul by a faithful counsellor often lasts for life. For Saul, the voyage without a pilot was becoming more tempestu-ous. Because a man has overmastered his conscience, so that he can sin in spite of its stings, it does not follow that he is happy in sinning. Bear witness ye, who have forsaken the lessons of your youth, have abandoned your Bible, have estranged yourselves from prayer, have run into ways which once you shunned with horror, and who nevertheless know that ye were never so wretched in your lives.

"The Spirit of the Lord departed from Saul, and an evil spirit from the Lord troubled [*terrified*] him." Relief must come from the very youth who is destined to replace him. Goliath, of Gath, defies the armies of the living God and dishonors their king. Relief must again come from the son of Jesse. The malicious rage and murderous intentions of Saul go on to worse crimes against the harmless and forgiving

David. The star of the abandoned king
pales its ineffectual fires. His frenzy breaks
out against the priesthood of God, and his
treachery practises mischief secretly against
his rival. Amidst these increasing sins and
sorrows, Samuel the prophet dies, and probably leaves no one on earth who can influence
the apostate king for good. We need not
wonder to see the last act run down rapidly
towards its catastrophe ; and this brings us
more directly to our special subject.

When men forsake the true God, they
seek direction and aid from idols, and sometimes from evil spirits. The more besotted
they are by sin, the more do their vain
curiosity and guilty foreboding lead them
to pry into the future, which an evil conscience prompts them continually to dread.
Here we find the origin of all augury, sooth-

saying, magic, witchcraft, and necromancy. They all involve a distrust and denial of the true God, and therefore were forbidden under heavy penalties by the Mosaic Law.

We are not permitted to say that all was imposture, either in the witch of former days, or (if I must use their own jargon) the *medium* of our own ; though in both nine parts out of ten may be referred to this source. As we know that there were real demoniacal possessions, we need not doubt that by a similar collusion with abandoned and impious men, Satan and his angels sometimes afforded a knowledge of things beyond human ken ; and this would be proper witchcraft. The alliance of what is absurdly called *Spiritualism* (I use the term under protest) with nervous disease, abnormal susceptibility and licentious passion, has been

sufficiently made out in our own day, to set
wise and virtuous persons on their guard.
In a period of great unbelief and crime such
extravagancies abound, just as noxious ver-
min crawl out at night.

As King of Israel, Saul had animadverted
in a stringent manner on these seducers, who
professed to hold commerce with the spirits
of the departed.   The presumption is, that
he had done this in his better day and under
the counsel of the great prophet; for mark
the connection : "Now Samuel was dead,
and all Israel had lamented him, and buried
him in Ramah, even in his own city.   And
Saul had put away those that had familiar
spirits and the wizards, out of the land."
But when his day began to decline, and tem-
pestuous clouds betokened an evening of despair, the agony of his soul craved some rev-

clation concerning the future. He was beset by enemies, and saw the Philistines, not merely at the doors, but within the citadel, and gaining on him every day. "And when Saul saw the host of the Philistines, he was afraid, and his heart greatly trembled." Prop after prop had been taken from him ; his skies shone lurid ; David had been driven away, and Samuel was dead. Greatly as he had offended against the God of his fathers, he still essayed to gain some light from his wisdom ; as we frequently see profligate men, in times of extreme fear, resorting to divine service and to the ministers of religion. But in vain. "And when Saul inquired of the Lord, the Lord answered him not, neither by dreams, nor by Urim, nor by prophets." This was perhaps the turning-point in his defection from the

true God. Before this, he probably might
have returned ; but now he consciously and
wilfully abandons Jehovah forever. In like
manner, we find all the leading devotees and
advocates of our modern necromancy to be
infidels. They forsake God before they sell
themselves to the devil. It is but a partial
glimpse which we can gain into the secret
throes and convulsions of a black and pow-
erful nature like Saul's. The woes of Orestes
and Œdipus, on the Grecian stage, could not,
in their original, have been more fearful. His
thoughts in tumult must have broken into
such ejaculations as these : All is over with
me ! The heavens above me are brass, and
the ear of God is deaf. No response comes
to me from the awful void. My foes increase
and there is no help for me in God. I will
betake me to other powers of nature, of

which I have heard. There is more than
one kingdom in the universe ; and perchance
there may be a turbulent satisfaction in ally-
ing myself with the principalities which fell.
At least, let me avail myself of their keener
insight.

"Then said Saul unto his servants, Seek
me a woman that hath a familiar spirit, that
I may go to her and inquire of her." The
clairvoyante whom they indicated lived at
a place named En-Dor ; and thither the
despairing monarch went in disguise, by
night, accompanied by two retainers. After
quieting the fears of the hag, he expressed
his desire to commune with one of the departed.

I cannot bring myself to believe, that the
spirits of just men made perfect can be
made to come and go at the bidding of

an unclean sorceress, or her diabolical master; and therefore I suppose the appalling event which followed was as truly a surprise to *her* as to *him*.

But let us return to our story. "Then said the woman, 'Whom shall I bring up unto thee?' And he said, 'Bring me up Samuel!'" These are the words for which we have been preparing and to which we shall return, after completing a few steps of the history. For "when the woman saw Samuel, she cried with a loud voice; and the woman spake to Saul, saying, 'Why hast thou deceived me? for thou art Saul.' And the king said unto her, 'Be not afraid: for what sawest thou?' And the woman said unto Saul, 'I saw gods ascending out of the earth.' And he said unto her, 'What form is he of?' And she said, 'An old man

cometh up, and he is covered with a mantle.
And Saul perceived that it was Samuel, and
he stooped with his face to the ground, and
bowed himself." The picture is shadowy
but complete ; a few touches go home to the
imagination and the heart ; as in great
sculpture, or some tragic situation in Æschy-
lus. The miserable king had his wish. The
hoary prophet had risen, though independ-
ently of the conjuring of the witch. From
those holy lips he heard his awful doom and
fell prostrate. Not many hours elapsed before the prediction was fulfilled. " To-mor-
row shalt thou and thy sons be with me."

But the truth to which your attention is
specially invited, and which is founded on
the king's reply, " Bring me up Samuel," is
this, that in times of affliction, remorse and
fear, our thoughts go back to the instruc-

tions and the teachers of our former years.
"Bring me up Samuel," means, Oh, let me see
once more the holy monitor of my youth;
let me again hearken to words of loving
wisdom from those lips; let me learn from
the only faithful friend of my throne, what
are my duty and my doom. The state of
his mind is made more clear by his own
words, after the apparition rose: "I am
sore distressed; for the Philistines make
war against me, and God is departed from
me, and answereth me neither by prophets
nor by dreams: therefore I have called thee,
that thou mayest make known unto me what
I shall do." In these unutterable sorrows,
he bethought him of Samuel. Chased as
by a demon, and harrowed by remembrances
of guilt, his mind went back, we may
suppose, to the first interview of his pastoral

youth, when Samuel communed with him in the privacy of the housetop.

There are moments in which the whole tapestry of past life seems to be unrolled, with all its colours of sadness, and especially that of guilt. It was such a moment with Saul. Looking back, as in a feverish delirium, he could descry along his burning track, every point at which he struck off into new wanderings. With every change in his dream, the figure of the prophet was mingled. At every crime, the expostulating look of the prophet comes back to him. "Bring me up Samuel," bursts from his parched lips. He does not ask for the companions of his pleasures, the instruments of his ambition, the guides of his devious errors; he asks for the sternest man he ever knew. If once he regarded his code as severe, and

his denunciations as fierce, he now longs for
him as the one who was true, uncompromis-
ing, and on the side of God. In days of trou-
ble, it is not our flatterers to whom we go.
Saul remembered that day of thunder and
lightning, when the prophet had shown his
friendship by declaring : " Moreover, as for
me, God forbid that I should sin against the
Lord in ceasing to pray for you : but I will
teach you the good and the right way." Perhaps he thought this adviser of his youth
could now do him some good, in his extremity. Children thus flee to their parents in
fear of storms ; and most of us have known
the hour when we felt safer near those who
were pious and benignant.

It is a most striking trait, that of all be-
ings, the one to whom Saul in anguish turns,
is the reprover of his sins. And the princi-

ple lies so deep in human nature, that every hearer has felt it tell upon his conscience as the narrative has proceeded ; nay, the hour is coming, when many a hearer, now careless in his sins, shall turn on his bed of poignant suffering, and groan—Bring me up Samuel !

No man can tell, during his days of hurried pleasure and sinful excitement, how he will be affected in the hour when his comforts have fled, when the vortex has stopped, and when he is thrown upon himself. "Jerusalem remembered in the days of her affliction and of her miseries all her pleasant things that she had in the days of old."* *Dulces moriens reminiscitur Argos.* In this moment of forlorn solitude, many pictures recur to the sickly mind of the heart-broken king. He sees the hills of Ben

* Lament. i. 7.

3

jamin, the house of Kish, the herds and pastures of his boyhood; the journey with his servant, when he dreamed of rebellion and witchcraft as little as of a crown; the ecstacy of inspiration when he seized and touched the harp of prophecy; and the manly exultation with which he returned from the field of trophies, met by the timbrel and the dance. How sad is the memory of joys which can never return! How desolating to recall times of purity, when we have become corrupted! But Saul's holiest remembrances gathered around the venerable head of Samuel. From his lips had flowed the teachings of wisdom, and his happiest days were when he lent to them a docile ear. Thoughtful hearer! you are already applying it to yourself. You likewise have memories, and you are forgetting the sermon while your mind lapses to those green fields of your country home, where, amidst hard but virtuous husbandry, or by the hearth of parents and grandparents, and brothers and sisters, (where are they now?) you "felt that you were happier than you knew." Since those days, you have tasted of the tree of the knowledge of good and evil, and your eyes have been opened. Yet you go back in thought to some ancient adviser, who told your incredulous youth how sad its manhood might become; and you have found it true.

I could with great respect and interest turn aside to address a few reminding words to the dull, cold ear of age. He who is overtaken by infirmity, and has reached the days in which to say, "I have no pleasure in them," is full of recollections; and among

these a special place is occupied by the lessons
and other privileges of former years. The
aged person indulges in tender reverie concerning the season when religious knowledge
came freshly home to the soul ; when the
house of God was a solemn place ; when
religious awakening shook whole assemblies ;
when youthful companions flocked into the
church ; when prayer was earnest, and when
Jesus himself seemed to be passing by. As
all the opportunities of your childhood and
youth will meet and confront you at the bar
of Christ, so it is likely they will come and
startle you even before that day. Only let
some great desertion, or bereavement, or
loss, or pain, or illness, or disabling stroke
come upon you, (it is conceivable,) while yet
you have no supports and consolations of
grace—only let some limb be benumbed,

some sense stopped up, some incurable mal-
ady fixed in your frame, some nervous trepi-
dation unfit you for life's joys—(it is not
impossible)—and your eyes will turn to former means of grace, to the church and bible of
your springtide, and to the voice of God,
which rung unheeded in your ears. Long before decrepitude, the language is often heard:
"How have I hated instruction, and my heart
despised reproof ; and have not obeyed the
voice of my teachers, nor inclined mine ear to
them that instructed me. I was almost in all
evil in the midst of the congregation and as-
sembly."* The sting in Saul's recollections
was *instruction disobeyed.* He had been reproved ; but "he that, being often reproved,
hardeneth his neck, shall suddenly be cut off,
and that without remedy." And the appre-

* Prov. v. 12–15.

3*

hension of this imminent execution was now causing him to shake with horror.

Samuel, the prophet, had fearlessly rebuked Saul; yet in extremity Saul cries, "Bring me up Samuel." He had been aggrieved by those faithful reproofs, but now the reprover is brought to mind. Thus, being dead he still speaketh; just as John the Baptist still spake in the conscience of Herod, causing him to see this second Elijah even in the gentle miracles of Jesus, and to say, "It is John the Baptist who has risen from the dead." Bring me Samuel, cries he who disregarded Samuel while living. And so it often is. The father and mother who taught you the right ways of the Lord, have been met by your contempt and disobedience. But the days are coming when their meek, remonstrant faces shall flit

before you, and when you will long to bring
them back, that you might learn from them
the secret of their happiness and their
power. Beside the tomb of your parents,
you will be ready to long that you could
bring them again, that you might bewail
your undutiful neglects, and make even this
tardy reparation for the dishonor you have
done them. For, what blessing of your better days is not associated with their persons
so closely that you cannot think of youthful
joys without thinking of *them*? And what
instructions can ever compare with those
which were the first, the simplest, and the
most loving? If you had the power of
raising the dead, in your hour of woe, your
language would not be, Bring me up the
ministers of my mirth — my comrades in
wassail and the dance—my flatterers, my

lovers, my deceivers, the partners of my avarice and my pomp, the serpents that twined about me and stung me ; but, Bring me up the "old man" covered with a mantle, whose gray hairs I brought down with sorrow to the grave! Bring me up *her*, who loved me even in my waywardness, who tried to counsel me even when I would not hearken, who comforted me in illness, and who died breathing prayers in my behalf! The feeling of the rich man in torment was natural; but such appeals of sinners to the other world are vain, "neither would they be converted though one rose from the dead." Should you enter some cavern, and from some gaping chasm behold the apparition of those honored forms, it would only be to hear what Saul heard, "Why hast thou disquieted me, to bring me up?" Why call us from our rest, to mourn anew over the sins which ye will not abandon?

Ministers of the gospel often lament in secret over the indifference with which their messages are heard, and sometimes they forecast a time, after their decease, when their words may come back to these hearers with a prevailing force. In this way, as well as others, dead ministers continue to preach. It is wise to cherish their memory. "Remember them . . . which have spoken unto you the word of God; whose faith follow." But times of distress particularly bring them to mind. Even while they live, they are often sent for in great haste, and alas! too late, by those who neglected them in days of health, but who now cry out for their guidance and prayers amidst the agonies of death. And when the faithful pastor has been dead many years, his warnings still linger in the mind of the ungodly, who, surrounded by the Philistines, entangled in the sins of a life-time, and awaiting unknown increase of terrors, earnestly cries, O that I could *now* hear what I *once* contemned! O for a day, an hour, of instruction from the father of my childhood, the counsellor of my riper years! Give me back my unheeded monitor—" Bring me up Samuel!"

Ah! my respected but unconverted hearers, we come to you, after many trials of preparation and with much consciousness of infirmity, sermon after sermon, Sabbath after Sabbath, month after month, year after year; we grow gray and feeble waiting on you with the Lord's message, which you will not consider; and then we die and you

are released from the distasteful reiteration
of warning and entreaty. God grant that
the day may not come when you shall gaze
on some marble and wish us back ; and
when echo shall seem to say with Samuel,
" Wherefore then dost thou ask of me, see-
ing the Lord is departed from thee, and is
become thine enemy." Suppose we could
return all ghastly to stand beside your
death-bed, we could bring you no gospel
which you have not rejected. Nothing will
have come upon you but that which we had
predicted. You have been forewarned ; so
was Saul. Hence, the prophet whom he
invokes, says to him : " And the Lord hath
done to him as he spake by me . . . . because thou obeyedst not the voice of the
Lord." " Because I have called and ye re-
fused ; I have stretched out my hand and

no man regarded ; but ye have set at naught all my counsel and would none of my reproof ; I also will laugh at your calamity. I will mock when your fear cometh ; when your fear cometh as desolation and your destruction cometh as a whirlwind, when distress and anguish cometh upon you. Then shall they call upon me, but I will not answer : they shall seek me early, but they shall not find me : for that they hated knowledge, and did not choose the fear of the Lord."

The scene changes in the 31st chapter, to the battle-ground of Mount Gilboa. Amidst the dust and turmoil of the fight, we behold a gory figure, taller than all about him, and scarcely taught to stoop, even in his despair. He is begirt with Philistines. There lie the corpses of Jonathan and his other sons.

Let us read, "And the battle went sore against Saul, and he was sore wounded of the archers. Then said Saul unto his armor-bearer, Draw thy sword and thrust me through therewith, lest these uncircumcised abuse me. But his armor-bearer was afraid. Therefore Saul took a sword and fell upon it." The prophet whom he called up had foretold it all. Even those who have loved us and exhorted us, must take God's side, and be witnesses against us, if we reject the counsel of God against ourselves. Be assured, my unpardoned hearers, unless Christianity is a fiction, days are coming in which the truths with which you now trifle will have acquired a portentous solemnity. How differently sounds the name of JESUS, now, in your moments of security . . . and in the chamber of death!

4

What an unmeaning object is the CROSS,
here, where you have no sense of danger . .
. . and what is its import yonder, at the
close of your career, when this only can
save you from hell! The whole intention
of these remarks has been to impress on you
a weighty reason for hearkening now to
the lessons of wisdom, because otherwise
you will turn to them with the instinct of
anguish in the hour of despair. Thus Jesus
weeps over Jerusalem, saying, " O, that thou
hadst known, even thou, the things that
belong to thy peace; but now they are
hidden from thine eyes!"

Great privileges do not secure salvation.
To *Christ* himself, some will say, "Hast
THOU not taught in our streets?" to whom
he will reply, "I never knew you!" Dear
hearer, the Mount at whose foot you stand

to-day, is not Gilboa, nor yet Sinai . . . it is Zion! Come, therefore, to Jesus, the Mediator of the new covenant, and to the blood of sprinkling, that "speaketh better things than that of Abel." Why will ye die, when salvation is at the door, and when we pray you in Christ's stead to be reconciled to God?